The New Bike

Written by
Marie Vinje

Illustrated by
Stephen Lewis

Lee is now six
and has a new bike.

She wants to show it
to her friend Mike.

But first she must
learn how to ride.

When Lee began,
Dad was right by her side.

**She fell many times,
but she did not cry.**

She got back on
for another try.

Lee is ready to go at last.
She pedals her bike onto the path,

up the hill,

across the bridge,

past the woods,

under a tree,

over leaves,

around a bend,

and through the gate.

Lee still has to learn
how to use her brake!